May Belle
AND THE Ogre

🍂 by Bethany Roberts 🍂
🍂 pictures by Marsha Winborn 🍂

DUTTON CHILDREN'S BOOKS · NEW YORK

To the Plot Luck Club, with love
—B.R.

To Lucia, for her faith, laughs, and Ogre-ish fun throughout
—M.W.

Text copyright © 2003 by Bethany Roberts
Illustrations copyright © 2003 by Marsha Winborn
All rights reserved.

CIP Data is available.

Published in the United States 2003 by Dutton Children's Books,
a division of Penguin Putnam Books for Young Readers
345 Hudson Street, New York, New York 10014
www.penguinputnam.com
Designed by Irene Vandervoort
Printed in Hong Kong/China   First Edition
ISBN 0-525-46855-2
1 3 5 7 9 10 8 6 4 2

Contents

One summer night,

May Belle painted her toenails.

Pink!

She had a pretty new hat.

So she put it on.

She had pretty new gloves.

She put them on, too.

Then she sat on her porch.

She sang this song:

"Oh! There's nothing like

A summer night

To make a May Belle

Feel all right!

Dee-diddle-dee-dum-dee!"

Suddenly she heard:

BUMP! BUMP! BUMP!

"Oo-oo-ooh!" said a scary voice.

"I want your pretty hat!"

"Not my pretty hat!" cried May Belle.

"OO-OO-OOH!" said the voice.

"Yipes!" said May Belle.

"Then take it!"

And she threw her hat

into the bushes.

Everything was quiet for a while.

But then she heard:

CLUMP! CLUMP! CLUMP!

"Oo-oo-ooh!" said a scary voice.

"I want your pretty gloves!"

"Not my pretty gloves!" cried May Belle.

"OO-OO-OOH!" said the voice.

"Yipes!" said May Belle.

"Then take them!"

And she threw her gloves

into the bushes.

For a while,

everything was still again.

But then she heard:

KA-THUMP! KA-THUMP! KA-THUMP!

"Oo-oo-ooh!" said a scary voice.

"NOW WHAT DO YOU WANT?"

cried May Belle.

Out of the woods stepped

a furry little ogre.

"OO-OO-OOH!" said Ogre.

"I want your pretty feet!"

"My feet? Never!" said May Belle.

May Belle looked at Ogre.

"Why, you are just a little ogre," she said.

"Shame on you for scaring me."

Ogre hung his head.

May Belle looked

at Ogre's big, dirty feet.

"I know what you need," she said.

She took Ogre by the ear.

She brought him into her house.

She gave Ogre a sudsy bath.

She scrubbed and scrubbed.

Then she painted his toenails.

Pink!

"My, what pretty feet I have!"

said Ogre.

"I don't need these anymore."

He gave back May Belle's hat

and gloves.

Arf!

"Here's one last touch,"

said May Belle.

She took the ribbon from her hat.

She tied a pink bow in his hair.

"Beautiful!" she said.

Ogre grinned.

Then he skipped off

into the bushes.

"Oo-oo-ooh!"

"Good night, Ogre!"

called May Belle.

May Belle sat on her porch
and sang.

"Oh! There's nothing like
A summer night
To make a May Belle
Feel all right!
Toes are pink,
The moon is bright,
Dee-diddle-dee-dum-dee!"

Blueberry Pie

One day,

May Belle was baking

a blueberry pie.

As she baked, she sang.

"Mix it, mix it, oh, my.

Roll it, roll it, by and by.

Bake it, bake it, blueberry pie.

I - LOVE - PIE!"

She took the pie

out of the oven.

She put it

on the windowsill to cool.

"I will read a book

while I wait," she said.

After a while,

BUMP! BUMP! BUMP!

Someone came and stole the pie

and gobbled it all up!

Soon May Belle came back

to the kitchen.

She saw her pie was gone.

"Someone took my pie,"

she grumbled.

"I wonder if that someone

has furry arms?

Well, I will bake another pie."

So she baked another pie.

And as she baked, she sang.

"Mix it, mix it, oh, my.

Roll it, roll it, by and by.

Bake it, bake it, blueberry pie.

I - LOVE - PIE!"

She took the pie out of the oven.

She put it on the windowsill to cool.

"I will read some more

while I wait," she said.

After a while,

CLUMP! CLUMP! CLUMP!

Someone came

and stole the pie

and gobbled it all up.

Grrr!

"Who is taking my pies?"

May Belle asked.

"I wonder if that someone

has big feet.

Well, I will find out."

So she baked another pie.

"Mix it, mix it, oh, my.

Roll it, roll it, by and by.

Bake it, bake it, blueberry pie.

I - LOVE - PIE!"

She took the pie out of the oven.

She put the pie

on the windowsill to cool.

But this time,

May Belle hid around the corner

and watched.

After a while,

KA-THUMP! KA-THUMP!

KA-THUMP!

Someone came

and stole the pie

and began to gobble it up.

"STOP!" cried May Belle.

"I want my pie!"

GOBBLE! GULP!

"But I ate it," said Ogre.

"Then you shall bake me another,"

said May Belle.

She took Ogre by the ear.

She led him into her kitchen.

"Mix," she said.

Ogre mixed,

and May Belle sang.

"Mix it, mix it,

oh, my!"

"Roll," she said.

Ogre rolled,

and May Belle sang.

"Roll it, roll it,

by and by!"

"Bake," she said.

Ogre baked,

and May Belle sang.

"Bake it, bake it,

blueberry pie!"

Soon the pie was ready.

"OH!" sang May Belle.

"I – LOVE – PIE!"

And she ate it all up,

every crumb.

Ogre watched.

"Yum," said May Belle.

"Oo-oo-ooh!" moaned Ogre.

"That looked good!"

"Oo-oo-ooh," said May Belle.

"I feel full!"

One night,

May Belle sat in the living room,

reading a book.

"This house is much too quiet,"

she said.

"I wish I had a friend

to keep me company."

May Belle sang this song:

"Oh, my little house is cozy,
All year long.
But oh, to have a friend with me
To sing this little song."

May Belle closed her eyes.

Suddenly she heard:

BUMP! BUMP! BUMP!

"I suppose you want

your toes painted,"

she called.

"No," said a voice.

May Belle closed her eyes again.

CLUMP! CLUMP! CLUMP!

"I suppose you want

a bow for your hair,"

she called.

"No," said the voice.

May Belle closed her eyes again.

KA-THUMP! KA-THUMP! KA-THUMP!

"I suppose you want

some blueberry pie,"

she called.

"No," said the voice.

"I just want to sing

your song."

"Come in, come in!"

cried May Belle.

Ogre came inside.

May Belle and Ogre sang.

"Oh, my little house is cozy,
All year long.
And now I have a friend with me
To sing this little song."

They did a snappy tap dance together.

SHUFFLE, BUMP!

SHUFFLE, BUMP!

SWISH!

Yip!

SWISH!

May Belle read her book to Ogre.

They popped popcorn.

They blew bubbles.

They painted pictures.

They played pirates.

"Whew!" said May Belle.

"I have never had so much fun!"

"Oo-oo-ooh!" sobbed Ogre.

"Now what do you want?"

asked May Belle.

"Do you want to stay?"

Ogre nodded his head.

"Oo-oo-ooh!" he sniffed.

May Belle smiled a smile

as wide as the moon.

"Then stay," she said,

"and be my friend!"

Ogre jumped up and down.

BUMP!

CLUMP!

KA-THUMP!

Then Ogre yawned.

He jumped into a dresser drawer.

May Belle tucked him in.

"Good night, Ogre," she whispered.

"ZZZ-ZZZ-ZZZ!" snored Ogre.

May Belle tiptoed to bed.

And just before she fell asleep,

she sang this song:

"Oh, a cozy bed,
A cozy night,
Friends forever—
It feels just right!
Dee-diddle-dee-dum-dee!"